I would like to dedicate this book twice. Once to my wonderful family. Second to my amazing friends. You have all believed in me, even if I haven't always seen it myself.

Zoë Davis

AN ELEMENT
OF MYSTERY

Short Stories and Poetry

AUSTIN MACAULEY PUBLISHERS™

LONDON • CAMBRIDGE • NEW YORK • SHARJAH

A CIP catalogue record for this title is available from the British Library.

ISBN 9781398439061 (Paperback)
ISBN 9781398439078 (ePub e-book)

www.austinmacauley.com

First Published 2022
Austin Macauley Publishers Ltd®
1 Canada Square
Canary Wharf
London
E14 5AA

Thank you to Austin Macauley Publishers, for my second book.

The Mystery of the
Red Diamond

With her dying breath, Lady Scarlett Diamond hid the envelope that would allow only the worthy heir to find the precocious Diamond family jewels.

Of all of the members of the Diamond family, Lady Scarlett Diamond was the most elusive. Historians knew little to nothing about her; the only documented fact was that she had died under mysterious circumstances and that her vast fortune, the Diamond family fortune, had disappeared at the same time. There were rumours abound that a letter had been written and secreted in a chimney stack. A letter that would not only explain what had happened on that fated day but that would also give the first clue to finding the fortune.

Many fortune hunters, glory hunters (vultures would be a better word) had searched in vain—not a sniff nay a whiff of this mysterious letter had ever been found. The loss of the family fortune had been lamented during the years. Not wanting to substantiate the claims, the family continued on spending money as they had always done; with nary a thought to the eventual consequence. This is why in the fall of 1867, on the brink of bankruptcy, the then lord and heir of the

Diamond legacy Lord Duncan took what was left of the fortune and disappeared, never to be seen again.

From then until this day, the Diamond family have lived on nothing but a name and misguided grandeur. One day, they hope their fortune will be restored.

Many years later…

A shoulder to the door was the only way to gain entry to the ancestral manor of the Diamond family. The hinges squealed in indignation at this unexpected use after years, so many years. The air was musty and had the rank undertones of mildew and decay, and then there was this presence, a deep presence that seemed to be rooted into the very foundation of the house itself. Henry Ottoman stood shivering in the vast entrance chamber, and next to him stood Mr Stone (the Diamond family lawyer).

"Vell, Meester Orttoman, zis is ze entrance chamber, zer are sieben."

Henry, whose German was non-existent, raised a quizzical eyebrow at this.

Mr Stone laughed a singularly unpleasant laugh and held up seven fingers. "Rooms leading off here, ze rooms are interconnected. If ve vere able to go up ze grand staircase you vould find ze study and master bedroom. Finally, zere is ze attic vich is vere ze servants' quvarters are. Now Meester Orttoman, are zere any qvestions as I am veery busy?"

Before Henry had had chance to reply, Mr Stone produced a sheaf of paperwork, riffled through and extracted a page, saying, "Zis is for you to zign and zen zee 'ouse and title are yours."

Henry took the proffered pen and signed once as he was and once again with his new ancestral title—Lord Henry Diamond.

That was when the trouble began...

Lady Diamond stood in the shadows, watching the transaction with a furrowed brow and her hands clasped together neatly in front of her; that accent though, there was something familiar about it. As she was about to leave, something caught her attention; an unfurling and furling pulsing mass of black that reverberated in the very centre of Mr Stone. Looking face on, it couldn't be seen but in peripheral vision, it stood stark and smelled of old evil. It was the type of evil that endured for millennia, the type of evil that hadn't been seen in living memory. Lady Diamond stood transfixed, half turned away, then she felt the mass turn and look straight at her. It should have caused a blackout, her soul being pushed away, forced to leave. However, the mass's edges softened and shimmered as it pulsed and moved forwards. Mr Stone's body gave a small jerk as the mass parted company. Once free of the body, it began to morph and contort. Out of the centre came a shrill lingering scream and a shadowy figure was flung forward. A man of middling height, shrewd and canny, Lord Charles Diamond had finally come back.

The temperature in the entrance chamber dropped and icicles began to appear on the bannisters of the once-grand staircase. Henry and Mr Stone shivered and their breath hung like mist in front of them.

"Whh-whh what happened, ho-ho-how ddd-dd-ddid I end up here?" He stared accusingly at Henry. "Ddd-dd-ddid you bring me here?" gasped Mr Stone.

Henry gave him an appraising look and said, "You brought ME here, a matter of some urgency, YOU said. You phoned me up in the middle of the night to tell me that I was the long-lost heir to the Diamond fortune and that as my lawyer, it was your duty to show me my mansion and discuss the terms of my inheritance."

Mr Stone stood staring as though he was trying to work something out, then he said slowly, "Hmmmmm, yes, I remember calling but then my mind is a blank, I phoned you and then I was standing here."

"Hang on a moment," cried Henry, "you were speaking in heavily accented English, yes, a strong German accent; where's that gone, sir?"

"Me, sir? I've never spoken with a German accent in my life," shouted Mr Stone indignantly.

Lady Diamond's shimmer dimmed ever so slightly then it glowed brightly as she recognised Charles; his outline and aura were becoming stronger as he shook himself out and raised himself to his full and intimidating height.

"Yes, yes, zat vas not a pleasant experience."

When his wife looked confused, he added, "Death, not as von vould imagine, you understand, and hell, vell of zat ve shall not zay."

The rejoice at the reunion was short-lived as Lady Diamond realised why her husband was back (although he had always said he would cheat death and return); he was back because Diamond manor had been passed onto the last full-blooded male in line to inheritance. Even in death, he didn't want the whereabouts of the fortune found; however, he didn't realise that secreted in the chimney stack was a clue to its whereabouts, that Lady Diamond had planted before her death, in hopes that it would release her into death's waiting arms and allow her some peace from the wickedness of her penultimate act in life (helping Charles hide the remaining fortune).

After Charles' gruesome and well-publicised death, she decided to write a letter which would direct the rightful heir to a single clue; if the heir was worthy, they would be able to decipher the coded message and find the treasure. On her deathbed, Lady Diamond hid the letter, hoping that she would be spared and allowed eternal peace. Alas! It was not meant to be because as the fabled pearly gates appeared, she felt herself being sucked down by what could only be likened to a tornado whirlwind. The winds deposited her insubstantial form back into the room she had just vacated, and as though she needed it, in front of her was conclusive proof that she hadn't been dreaming. Her now-lifeless body slumped forward and began to shimmer and then disappeared. She knew what she must do, so she watched and waited. Centuries passed and her hope began to fade that she would ever see the rightful heir returned.

Henry and Mr Stone glared at each other, unsure how to proceed. As they were about to start shouting again, a ghastly figure of a man appeared and when he spoke, it was in a heavily German accented English.

"Zo, you are ze pup zat zey zay is my rightful heir. You vill vish it vasn't zo, I theenk. Eef you vant to prove me ozervise, you need to 'urry, I vill be vatching closely. Yes, good luck, you vill need it, hahahahhahahahhahahah!"

As the ghastly figure receded into the background, a bright white light shone out and it spoke in a soft voice, most unlike the man before. "Please, listen carefully and act immediately. In the master bedroom lies a chimney stack; inside, there is a loose brick, pull it out. You will find a folded piece of paper. Follow the instructions inside, they will help you find the lost fortune." With that, the white light disappeared and the two men were left staring in disbelief at the ceiling.

It was as if a light switch had been flicked inside Henry's head. The mention of a chimney stack resonated in the back of his memory, some long and forgotten memory. As Henry started forward, Mr Stone shot a warning arm out in front of him, halting Henry in his tracks.

"You're not actually going to go and check, are you? How do we know we can trust that, that blob?"

Henry just stared. How was he going to explain a feeling, an instinct perhaps?

"I don't know why," he said slowly, "I can't even explain it. I have a feeling that we can trust the blob. Look, I'm not asking you to come with me, you can leave anytime. I'm going to trust my instincts and go and check out the chimney stack in the master bedroom." With that, Henry turned on his heel and marched off towards the grand staircase.

Mr Stone hesitated for about half a second and hurried towards the door. He stopped and looked at the lone figure of the young man moving across the landing. He sighed, turned towards the stairs and began to follow Henry.

A creak on the stairs told Henry that Mr Stone was following him. He smiled and stopped, allowing Mr Stone time to catch up. Silently, the two men turned and faced the bedroom door. Henry took a deep breath and turned the handle; the door swung open with the merest hint of a squeak. Henry stood on the threshold and started patting the wall with his hand, trying to locate the light switch. His wandering fingers eventually found it, and a soft click and flair of light illuminated the room, showing it in all its beauty.

The room was a stunning snapshot of Edwardian décor and tasteful wallpaper. A sharp intake of breath stirred Henry from his reverie; he turned to see Mr Stone drumming his fingers against his arm. Henry moved into the room and went towards the chimney. There was an intense hum in the room that made the very air vibrate, it was like the room was holding its breath in anticipation of the secret it had withheld in its depths. Henry knelt in front of the cavernous fireplace and started patting his pockets. In his right-side pocket, he found a book of matches and with trembling fingers he withdrew and struck a match; with a shaking hand he cupped the flame so it wouldn't go out and reached up into the gloom. With his heart beating a violent tattoo in his chest, Henry searched the base of the chimney, he moved into the dis-used fireplace and proceeded to search the soot ridden walls. With a leap of excitement, he saw a piece of paper wedged into a crack in the masonry work. Henry stretched up and began to carefully tug and twist the paper. A tense few minutes elapsed until it came free. Clutching the square of paper to his chest, as though it was most precious, Henry extricated himself from the fireplace. He beckoned Mr Stone over and began to unfold the small square of paper; it was only folded twice and covered in small cramped characters front and back.

Dear sir,

Congratulations to you, my one and true heir. Over the years, our families fortune has dissipated, and many say this is because of a thief who ransacked our family estate, here in fact. This is all true, but the facts have been twisted and indeed fabricated to suit the perpetrator's own ends. The estate was ransacked and the vaults emptied but not by a common thief, it was the then Lord Diamond, my own dear husband Charles. He hid the fortune in an undisclosed place, and unfortunately, never lived long after the incident to enjoy the wealth to its fullest as an incident occurred that resulted in his rather gruesome demise. I shall say no more of that incident. My own end is drawing closer. I can't reveal the fabled X on the map but I shall divulge a clue that will lead to another and hopefully set you in good stead to find our fortune. Know this, however, when you reveal yourself to the house, my Charles's spirit will descend again to prevent you from finding his fortune. You shall know him by his peculiar accent, but please be wary, he isn't benign; quite malevolent, in fact. Good luck, my heir, be swift in your actions and enjoy your fortune.

Lady Scarlet Diamond x

Henry stared at the paper, not daring to believe what he had read. He re-read the letter, there wasn't, however, any mention of the clue hinted at in the letter. Lady Diamond stood in the corner of the room, quietly observing, willing with all her might that he would notice the tiny arrow in the corner of the page indicating that the clue was just below them in the family room. This would prove again that he was a worthy heir. Lady Diamond smiled to herself and melted away into the foundations again.

Henry was still desperately scanning the letter for any indication of a clue when his eyes found a tiny arrow in the corner; so small it was easily overlooked. He resisted the urge to punch the air, remembering the warning about Charles. He showed the arrow to Mr Stone (Henry was grateful for the older man's presence) and muttered in his ear "Do you have the floor plans with you?"

Mr Stone nodded and produced the plans from his slimline leather briefcase. Between them, they cleared a space and spread the plans out.

"OK, we are here in the master bedroom. What is directly below us?"

Mr Stone frowned for the briefest of seconds and then hitched on his 'estate agent' face. "Well, we are here in the master bedroom," indicating the room on the plans, he carefully lifted the top of the plans to reveal the lower floors, "and the family room is directly below us."

Suddenly, Mr Stone yelped and jumped out of the way, as they watched fiery letters forming across the floor plans, spelling *GET OUT!* Underneath, a large C was all the signature given. The words glowed brightly for a few minutes and then consumed the plans in fire. A cackling could be heard echoing around the corners of the room then that terrible voice sounded again.

"My fair varning to you, by grace you have ten minutes to get out of my house."

Mr Stone paled even further and clutched at his heart. Henry, however, shouted, "Never! This is my house and I will find my fortune," then more quietly, "come on, Mr Stone, let's get down to the family room and see what we can find."

Mr Stone, however, looked quite incapable of moving as he stared in horror at the floor plans. A long high whimper escaped him and he bolted to the door, fairly flew down the stairs and as he fled into the night, Henry thought he heard "Vun down, vun to go" accompanied by a soft chuckle.

Finding the treasure with someone was far more appealing than being on his own, but never the less, Henry stalked down the stairs and silently made his way across the hallway to the door marked 'family room'.

Before he could enter, a voice spoke directly in his ear, "Well done, Henry. When you enter the room, go straight across to the serving tables on the left-hand side. There, you will find a drawer. Inside it, you will find the next clue. Good luck and hurry."

With a shaky but deep breath, Henry entered the family room. The door shut with a thud behind him and that terrible voice sounded again, "You leetle fool, you'll nezer get your handz on my fortune. I, the last heir, back to exact revenge on zose fools who locked me away. Zere deaths shall be payment for years lost, incarcerated in zat dark place as hot and fiery as hell, know zat your death vill sate my appetite for death a leetle vhile, vhilst I track down zose ozer imbeciles."

A dark, pulsing energy emanated from the shadowy figure as it materialised in the centre of the room, and for the first time, Henry stood face-to-face with his great, great, great, great uncle Charles; a foreboding man of middling height dressed in a light-grey suit, with a black waistcoat, highly polished spats and a narrow-brimmed hat. He had sharp eyes and a small goatee that couldn't quite hide his weak chin.

Drawn to full height, he stared imperiously at Henry, who couldn't help but quail under that frightful gaze.

As he stood there, Henry fought every urge to run as fast as he could away from the room, the house, that man, for even dead Charles cut an intimidating figure that was used to being obeyed without question. Just as Henry's resolve was weakening, the bright blob appeared in his prereferral vision and the sight strengthened him. He pulled himself up to full height and made a slight bow to Charles, saying, "Sir, I have been directed presently to ignore everything in this room and proceed across to the serving tables. This I shall do as I am the rightful heir and will be claiming my fortune today."

With that, Henry turned in the direction of the serving table; he took one step forward and then another, a shrill howl sounded in his ears but Henry didn't dare look around to see the source of the noise as it would be counterproductive to his final plan.

The shrill howl and coldness of the room subsided but with dogged determination, Henry continued in case of a reappearance by the late Lord of Diamond. Henry contented himself with a quick glance around to check the surroundings; all was clear. After all his bravado, Henry was barely standing on his weak and violently shaking legs. Deciding to sit instead of falling down, Henry devoted a few moments to a cascade of questions and thoughts racing around his mind, all vying for his attention. First and foremost was, how to avoid a vengeful ghost who was out for your blood.

"The only way is to get to the fortune before he does," whispered the voice, the voice Henry had come to rely on.

With renewed determination, Henry rose to his feet and quickly covered the distance between himself and the serving table. He quickly located the drawer needed and with deftly nimble fingers, Henry removed a minutely folded piece of yellowing paper. Henry re-scanned the room before unfolding the next clue.

My heir,

You found the next clue. Congratulations.

To glean more information, you must seek out our family history.

Good luck.

Henry re-read the clue again until he had it memorised, he then retrieved the matches from his pocket, struck a match and set light to the clue. As the flame flared, a new message came into view:

A smart idea, my heir,

Fire is our greatest weapon.

As the flames licked their way up the corners of the paper, Henry felt their warm glow in his chest and it emboldened him to continue the search.

Silently, Henry made his way across the hallway and down a side corridor. He turned left and a gasp escaped him as he came face-to-face with a beautifully carved door depicting a vast book case with hundreds of intricately designed books, but there wasn't a door handle in sight. Henry stood and stared at the door willing it to divulge the secrets. After a time, he took several paces back and it was then that the clue came into view; individual words had been underlined forming a question 'What is our greatest weapon?'

As Henry thought, the answer swam hazily into view at the forefront of his mind; **Fire**, the secret message on the clue spoke of fire being our greatest weapon. Quickly, Henry scanned the titles and he finally located one on fire. Henry pressed on the book gently and with a soft click, the vast door swung open. Teetering on threshold, Henry had to take a moment before entering, such was the magnitude of the library. Books covered every inch of space, floor-to-ceiling book cases against every available wall. Books on every known subject, civilisation, religion—it was all there. Ancient ladders stood propped against the side of one such bookcase. Henry would have happily holed up in the library never to leave again, but he knew that he must finish what had been started. With crashing realisation, Henry understood that he didn't know where to start. Family history—it was a fairly broad topic; the clue had only disclosed how to get through the library door. Henry spun on his heel when he heard a genteel cough behind him; what he faced now was nothing short of breath-taking.

A young woman shrouded in a grey cloak spoke, "Patience, I couldn't hint too much in the note in case it was found. We're safe in here though, my Charles never appreciated the knowledge accumulated in here and as such it can be used against him. Our family history lies in the tomes over there, the dates are chronological." She stopped speaking abruptly, a hand appeared next to her, it roughly grabbed her arm and she was dragged with a look of silent fear through nothing and completely disappeared.

"Vell, vell, I now know how you haf been zo very successful in hunting my fortune. I find now zat my own vife haz been consorting vith ze enemy. She vill be dealt vith forthwith, but what oh vhat to do viz you?" An evil cackle erupted through the silence like thunder. "I haf decided, you vish to stay in zis library, vell, vish granted."

With that, the library door slammed and with a sinking heart, Henry knew this grand library would become his tomb.

Lady Diamond knew the price she would have paid for this betrayal if they had both been alive and, although Charles was dead, his temper when in a towering rage was still terrible to behold. She instinctively flinched when he returned from the library. The cold, distant look was far more intimidating than the stormy rage that had coloured their married days.

"Wha-what did you do?" she asked, but Charles ignored her and floated away.

He delighted in the torment it was causing; with each passing query, the plea became stronger. Charles had decided that as he couldn't hurt her physically anymore, well, refusing to answer her or even acknowledge that she was there was the next best thing.

Henry pondered and thought, thought and pondered and still couldn't see where the family's history lay. He had scoured the shelves of the book cases in a vain attempt to try and procure the secrets lost to time but to no avail. In a vain attempt to restore some order to his jumbled, confused mind, Henry resorted to pulling all the books off the shelf, reasoning that as he put them back in a tangible order, he would find the illusive book. Over the next few hours, Henry removed hundreds of books and as he emptied a shelf, he then put them back in order. As the grip of bone-weary tiredness struck, he reached out to remove a volume called *Lords Genealogy*. A click and rumble exploded through the silence. As Henry leapt back in shock, the whole bookcase shook and then swung forward, revealing a doorway. As Henry stepped into the doorway, light flared on either side and as the gloominess evaporated a long stone passageway became clear. Tentatively, Henry began to make his way down the passageway, lights illuminating every few feet, the walls had an iridescent slimy glow and a strong smell of damp permeated the air. Henry continued along the passage, it suddenly took a sharp left and began to slope down and as Henry followed it, he became aware that he was walking in water; just a trickle to begin with but it steadily became a torrent that made it harder and harder to move through. For over an hour, he battled through the flooding, completely submerging several times, eventually making it to the other side. Henry flopped down there and then he slept.

Henry didn't know how long he slept for and would have probably slept longer if not for the deep rumbling in his stomach. He started, suddenly realising that he hadn't eaten anything in over 36 hours. Henry unclipped the buckle on his bag and withdrew a granola bar and a bottle of water. He ate quickly and then got up, dusted himself off and started up the slope. As he climbed, Henry felt cleaner, fresher air wash over him, cooling his sweaty brow and clammy body. After what felt like an age, Henry saw a door up ahead. Fatigue threatening to overcome him, Henry stopped and gulped down the last precious mouthfuls of water, wiping his mouth with the back of his hand.

Henry set off once again. He hurried forward and quickly covered the distance between himself and the door. Hand on the door handle and heart in mouth, Henry pushed the handle down and slipped through the small gap created, he found himself in an expansive study. As his eyes got used to the glaring sunlight that was filtering through the partially drawn curtains, Henry tentatively moved into the room and looked around. Unsure of what he was looking for, he tried in vain to remember the previous clue; 'You must seek out our family history'. He had pulled a book called *Lords' Genealogy* hurriedly. Henry went to the bookcase and scanned the shelves for a copy of *Lords Genealogy*. Nestled in the bottom, in left-hand corner, rested the genealogy. Henry's fingers gently grasped the tome and deftly removed it from the shelf. As the book was opened, a piece of paper fluttered out and was neatly caught by Henry before it hit the ground. With shaking fingers, Henry unfolded the paper and stared intently at the inscription.

My heir,

Congratulations on finding your way through the secret passage. To find the next clue, proceed to the conservatory and look in the place that sees no light.
Good luck.

Henry re-read the clue and then struck a match which set the paper alight. Hurrying across the room, Henry slid the door across and stepped onto the floor boards with a slight squeak. He quickly dashed across the hallway, heading towards the conservatory.

Charles was feeling discomforted, he had an unpleasant feeling that Henry was no longer in the library. He had reasoned and reasoned with himself that it was nye on impossible as there was no escape from the library. Of course, it wasn't a room that he had frequented much while he was

24

alive, but still, as he pored over the floor plans that the unfortunate Mr Stone had left behind, he found there was no way out of the library. Just to appease his troubled mind, Charles decided to check on Henry and (having checked that his wife was indeed resting) without further ado, he passed like grey mist through the wall.

Instantly, Lady Diamond was alert; she dematerialised and rematerialized in the library. With the wave of her hand, the books instantly leapt back onto the shelves and the bookcase closed with a quiet click. Lady Diamond concentrated intently on Henry's face and began to metamorphose into him. She then lay down on the couch and slowed her breathing down. Just in time, it seemed, as Charles appeared in the doorway and cast an eye over the room. He breathed a sigh of relief as he saw 'Henry' lying prone on the couch. Meanwhile, Henry had arrived at the conservatory.

Peering into the room, Henry saw that the conservatory had been converted into a mini-greenhouse; discarded pots lay strewn across the floor as well as dusty tables and potting tables. But where didn't receive any light? He pondered this thought as he entered the room. Looking around, everywhere seemed light and airy. The only place that wouldn't receive any sunlight would be underground, but no, surely not? Fruitlessly, Henry searched under the tables and potting stations and apart from several large, gangly spiders that had made their homes under there, he didn't find anything. As one of the spiders scuttled across the floor having been dislodged from the pot it had been living in, Henry's eyes followed it and in doing so, he spied in the corner a large planter that didn't actually have a plant in it. Peering into it, Henry couldn't see the bottom. Without any other options Henry climbed into the planter and disappeared below the brim. Hanging on by his fingertips, Henry still couldn't reach the bottom, so with a muttered oath under his breath, he shut his eyes tight and let go.

Henry dropped around two feet and landed hard on a beaten earth floor. The tunnel to Henry's right had a low ceiling, so, getting down on his knees, Henry crawled a short way and entered the subterranean basement of the conservatory. Brushing dirt from his knees, Henry struck a match and held it high to throw some light into the room. On the singular table in the room lay a letter, yellowed with age and brittle to the touch. As Henry began to read the letter, he yelped and dropped the match as the flames began to burn his fingers. As if in slow motion, Henry watched the lit match drop. Out of instinct, he made a great swipe and managed to knock the match off course and it landed harmlessly on the ground where it guttered and then went out. After a few moments, Henry's breathing slowed and he took a few deep, steadying breaths.

In the last guttering moments of the match, Henry had seen a stump of a candle in its holder. Moving across the floor, sightlessly, using his hands as a guide, Henry made it to sideboard. He felt along the sides and eventually felt the handle of the candle holder. Putting his hand in his pocket, Henry removed the book of matches. One strike, two strikes, on the third strike the match lit and flared. Carefully, Henry lit the candle then moved back towards the table. Without further ado, Henry read the clue on the letter.

You are closer than ever, my heir,

Proceed to the back of this room, you will find a door leading into the cemetery. Make your way to the family crypt. There seek out the final step and inside will be The Final Step.

Good luck as always.

By the light of the candle, Henry made his way to the back of the room. As he squeezed through the narrow doorway, Henry crushed the clue in his fist. As it disintegrated, he blew out the candle and made his way across the graveyard by the light of the full moon.

The graveyard was overgrown and tangled, this made the going very tough, but Henry hacked his way through with a combination of brute force and squeezing through small gaps. Henry moved deeper through the undergrowth; tangled bind weed surrounded every grave stone, owls hooted in the distance and bats screeched as they swooped and searched for fireflies in the night air. Henry continued on through the graveyard stopping every so often to disentangle himself from the weeds, when suddenly...

Ahhhhhhhhhhhhhhhhhhhhhh!

Charles screamed at the top of his voice. How could this have happened to him; he who had planned for so long, even cheated death to achieve it, and now to be thwarted at the last turn by his wayward wife and of course that young upstart Henry? No, he would have to think of something far more creative to get rid of them, especially as Henry had found a way out of the library. Charles returned to the library carrying a length of rope which he deftly twisted into a slipknot lasso. the first Lady Diamond knew about Charles having returned was when a length of rope tightened around her body, rendering her incapable of moving, Charles quickly secured the rope to an iron ring mounted in the wall.

"Vun down, vun to go, and zis time my elusive friend, I vill be triumphant."

Cackling, Charles melted into the background, leaving Lady Diamond to her futile struggles against her bonds.

Eventually, hot and sweating, Henry arrived at the crypt. He had the unpleasant feeling that he was being watched, so with a deep-set uneasiness, Henry pulled aside the trailing ivy and pushed the stone door in. As it swung open, he saw a set of stone steps leading down. Not wanting to close the door entirely, he left it ajar and trailing his right hand along the wall, he made his way down the stairs. Henry's hand nudged a lantern which crunched against the stone work. As he lit a match, he managed to narrowly avoid being pierced by the spear shaft that had just come whizzing down the stairs. Henry leapt sideways, rolling down the last few steps and crashing with a sickening thud into a stone coffin. Before Henry knew what was happening, he was lifted into the air and deposited in the coffin he had just crashed into.

As the light was shut off by the lid being slid over his head, he heard, "Ah, ze leetle boy vas close but not close enough. Enjoy your eternal rest vith your ancestors, hahahaha!" And with that, the lid slammed shut and Henry was trapped.

Charles resisted the temptation to do a little victory dance as he hadn't won yet, there was still the small matter of retrieving the fortune. Charles returned to the house and went up to the attic. There, he removed a small ornate key from the hook secreted in the nook just below the pane glass window.

Henry tried to remain calm and reminding himself to breathe, he thought through his options; all of which looked bleak. Shifting himself down slightly, Henry moved his arms into a classic press-up position and attempted to move the stone lid. Muscles straining and rapidly running out of air, Henry fought against the panic rising in his chest. Panicking would get him nowhere. As Henry tried to draw a breath, adrenaline took over coursing through his veins and his foot kicked out reflexively and a stone moved. Suddenly, the side of the coffin crumbled and Henry rolled out, gasping for breath. Without a moment to lose and profusely thanking the inventor who thought of a fail-safe if someone was buried without being dead, scrambling along the edges of other coffins, Henry made his way down the crypt and finally arrived at the final step. He dropped to his knees, hands fluttering out in search of the final clue.

In triumph, Charles brandished the key at the lock of an old chest, quite unremarkable to look at, which made it the perfect place to hide such a valuable commodity…

Henry's searching fingers eventually encountered a small brass key which he inexplicably knew fitted into the small lock hidden on the stone figure adorning the coffin behind him…

Charles fitted the key in the lock…

Henry fitted the key in the lock…

Turning the key, a click resonated through the room. In eager anticipation, the lid was opened and a howl of fury escaped…

Turning the key, a click resonated through the room. In eager anticipation, the lid was opened and a gasp of wonder…

A tornado whirlwind ripped through the attic, picking up Charles's furious form which fought and writhed against the inevitable, as he was dragged through the thin veil that keeps this world from the next.

He screamed, "I vill get my revenge!"

The bonds holding Lady Diamond slackened and then disappeared. She hurriedly moved through the room, arriving at the crypt where she saw Henry kneeling, with his head bowed. In front of his eyes were riches beyond his wildest dreams.

"Congratulations, Henry. I admit to being concerned for a while earlier, I thought that Charles had got the best of us, but you persevered and unravelled each clue. Each time proving that you are indeed a worthy heir for the title and fortune. By finding the fortune you have also sent Charles back to the great beyond and for that, I thank you profusely. My time is near, I shall be able to slip through the veil and stay on the side of the dead. You have released me; again, I thank you for that."

A white light shined down and settled on Lady Diamond. A radiant smile lifted her features and a sigh of contentment stole through her as she sparkled and then disappeared.

In years to come, Henry was unsure how best to explain how he had found the family fortune; had he truly followed a trail of clues leading to the crypt? There were news appearances and newspaper crews hanging around, people everywhere wanted the full story; what was he going to do with his new-found fame and fortune, did he believe that it was one of his ancestors who had stolen the fortune in the first place?

Henry decided it was best to keep quiet on the exact details that had transpired. All the world needed to know was that the fortune had been found.

Henry held a small private ceremony to commemorate the late Lord and Lady Diamond by unveiling a statue in their honour. This he hoped would appease the vengeful spirit of Charles Diamond, but as with any spirit you can never tell. Henry just had to hope and pray that the gesture would be appreciated.

The Monster Under the Bed

I am the darkness,
The shadows lurking in the corner,
The skeleton in your closet,
The monster under your bed.

There is a monster under my bed,
Its name is depression;
No one can see it,
Not even me.

I can feel it though;
It makes me feel small,
It makes me feel sad...

There is a monster under my bed,
Its name is anxiety;
No one can see it,
Not even me.

I can feel it though;
It makes me feel small,
It makes me feel scared...

What if I shone a light?
At the monster under my bed;
Then I would be able to see it,
So, would you,
Anxiety, depression…

Every monster has a name,
One day so will mine,

BUT…

Monsters are scared of light,
And of being seen.

Monster, you have no hold on me,
Now I can see you,
Everyone can see you.

I hold that light,
Keep it close,
For when the monster comes,
I'll show it to them.

The monster shrinks,
Becomes so small,
It hardly seems scary at all.

So, the next time your monster comes,
Remember,
A light shows them
For what they truly are.

Small,
Insignificant,
It doesn't define you,
That monster will learn,
It can't beat YOU.

The Circus

Roll up, roll up,
The cry goes around the town,
Excitement palpable,
The circus, the circus.

Wonder and intrigue,
What was that?
Strong men, bulging muscles,
How do they do that?

There's the big top,
A striped tent,
One like no other,
The circus centre.

Tightrope, trapeze,
The high-wire,
The audience like ants,
Watch in awe at the acrobats.

Clowning around,
Men and women in bright jumpsuits,

Covered in grease paint,
Wobbling around the ring.

Piled high on tiny bikes,
They crash into foam walls,
Juggling unimaginable objects,
Skills un-rivalled.

Out comes the ring master,
Top hat swept off in a bow to the audience,
Cheers and clapping sound through the tent,
The audience talk excitedly of what they have seen.

The circus, the circus,
The traveling troupe leave for another year,
Onto a new site,
New audiences to amaze.

Soon the cry of,
Roll up, roll up,
Will be heard again,
Only 365 days to go.

Stars

What are the stars?
Star signs?
Giant balls of gas?
Souls of loved ones watching over us?

Cancer, Leo,
Sagittarius, Capricorn,
Taurus, Pisces,
Stars tell the future.

Virgo, Scorpio,
Aquarius, Gemini,
Libra, Aries,
Stars tell the past.

Held in fascination,
Held in reverence;
Stars guide our lives,
Relationships, jobs.

Dotted in the sky,
Dancing between planets,

Stars are born;
Live and die.

Hurtling through the cosmos,
Billions of miles away,
Wish on a falling star,
Watch it soar.

Stars give life;
Life to the universe,
The vast emptiness of space
Watched since the dawn of time.

Man has always watched the stars,
For they show life;
Images in that unhospitable place,
Bridge the gap.

Those destined for the stars,
Will live for eternity,
To play among the planets,
And watch us on Earth.

Stars,
Giant balls of gas?
Or loved ones watching over us?

Anger

Anger is borne of pain,
It becomes destruction,
It eats you up,
And devours you whole.

Anger can suck you in,
Holds you tight,
It won't let you go,
All through the day and night.

Holding onto anger,
Is easy to do,
The harder thing,
Is to let it go.

Letting go
Means facing your anger,
Facing your anger
Can mean facing your pain.

Changing what you can,
Accepting what you can't,

Realising you must move forwards
'Fore that begins paving the way.

Forwards is where
You are heading now,
Forwards to
Happiness.
Future happiness,
V.s. anger's destruction,
Sometimes you need to be
Shown how to let go.

Write it down,
Draw a picture,
Screw it up,
Burn it.

Whatever helps,
Don't let anger's destruction
Hold you much longer,
Set yourself free.

Press-Ganged into the Navy

September 1805
Bleurgh

Walter's stomach roiled and his head pounded; he'd never had a hangover this bad. How much must he have drunk last night? His wife was going to kill him.

There was a sharp tang of salt in his nostrils and he was dimly aware of shouting going on around him, he decided that he must have stumbled along from the tavern to the dock and passed out there. There was a swaying and dipping motion beneath him that was getting worse the longer it went on. Walter knew that he must get up but he could barely open his eyes, he really wished that the dock would stop swaying. Now that his nose was used to the scent of salt, it was picking up a distinct mustiness, the sharp smell of sweat and damp wood. Walter's heart began to race and he felt himself break out into a cold sweat, dread filling his chest and threatening to engulf him in its hopelessness.

Fear was taking the lead this time; it was tearing around Walter's brain, leaving no room for any other emotions. What was going to happen to him, to his wife, his new-born baby? Fear was reminding him of the horror stories about the pressgangs that would go around the taverns, looking for men and boys who were already worse the wear for drink, and coercing them into joining the navy, tricking them into taking the king's coin. Walter was trying to sort through his foggy memories of the night before but fear was trying to prevent him from doing that, it was clouding every memory. Walter could feel the fear rising through him in uncontrollable waves, racing through his brain and making the adrenaline surge 'round his body. Walter's other emotions were trying to regain some control but to no avail. Fear was the strongest now; if it had its way, then this feeling of fear was going to rule him for however long he was on this ship.

Anger swiftly followed his fear, white hot burning anger; anger at the unknown person or persons who had done this to him. It was this, this anger that drove his fear away, and allowed the memories of the night before to come flooding forwards. Walter had finished work at the factory, he and a mate had decided to go for a drink at the local tavern and a group of sailors had come in and started talking of the high life on the sea. Walter had asked questions, shown an interest. The sailors kept buying him drinks, the more he drank the better the idea of the sea sounded. He took the last swallow of his drink and almost choked. Walter spat out a coin with the king's head on it, the sailors had cheered and told him that he would be joining them on board, going to sea. He had tried to leave, to say there had been a mistake—a pain on his head and the feeling of sinking into the abyss. Was it anger at the unknown sailors or anger at himself for showing an interest in the stories of glory at the high seas?

The next emotion to come sickened him to his core, because he felt joy, joy that he would be able to help defend his home, his country. The navy had always held a fascination for him, except when he pictured himself in the navy, he was smartly dressed in a uniform, he had enlisted himself, walked aboard not dragged—the adventure he had always wanted.

Feelings of guilt washed over him next, overwhelming guilt, extinguishing everything else. Who knew how long he would be gone for, would he even come back? What would happen to his wife, the woman he loved the most? How would she survive without him? Would she think he had just abandoned her? Oh God, if she couldn't pay the rent, how much leeway would she get? Would she end up in the poor house? Would his baby end up in a poor house orphanage? These terrible scenarios shrouded his brain in utter despair. If he made it out of this alive, he would never stop searching until he found them again, even if he had to work every day to buy his family's freedom from that dreadful place. Sadness began to come now; it was all he could do to not cry out with the feeling of it all rising up in his chest like a sickness. He knew he couldn't show any weakness; if they thought he was weak, it would finish him for sure. The sadness mingled with the guilt and created an empty black hole of despair in the pit of his stomach. All he could see was his poor, gentle and fragile wife having to throw herself on the mercy of the parish poor house, a place many would rather die than go to. His baby having to grow up in that place, a place where he was likely to die due to lack of proper care and nutrition—nutrition he should get from his mother, which he would be denied because she would have to work in order to stay there.

He felt a pair of strong hands grab him by the shoulders and lift him bodily up, along with the barked order of "Show a leg, sailor, Cap'n wants to see you." As the hands let go of him, Walter fought to keep himself upright, forcing his eyes open to look blearily around him.

"Where am I, how did I get here?" he managed to croak.

There was a mumbled reply from his right but his mind was in a such whirl that he didn't hear the answer. As if in a trance, Walter allowed himself to be steered up a set of wooden steps and out onto the rain-lashed deck, not that he noticed any of this. Stumbling along the deck, Walter heard laughter but wasn't sure if it was directed at him. After what felt like an age, they arrived at the captain's day cabin. A giant fist was raised and three loud knocks resonated. Walter felt a hand in the small of his back as he was pushed into the room.

The captain stood resplendent in his immaculate uniform.

"New recruit, Cap'n; a willing sailor who took the king's head last night."

A glare in Walter's direction made it clear to not contradict him, the captain turned on his heel to look Walter up and down with a critical eye.

"Is this true, Sailor? Are you a willing recruit? Weren't pressganged, were you?"

Walter swallowed and his courage failed him, he nodded twice and then after a moment's hesitation, he shook his head once.

"Excellent, make your mark here."

As soon as Walter had made a shaky cross in the book, the captain's demeanour changed—he became more business-like as he laid down the law and consequences to be expected for any discrepancies that were made. Once the captain made sure that Walter understood the rules, he assigned him a job as a Gunner's Mate. Walter was then sent to the gunner's deck.

As busy as Walter was by day, or night depending, it was during his off-time that his mind would wander to thoughts of home and where his wife and son would be now, whether they were OK?

Six weeks passed without a whiff nay a sighting of the enemy. On the night watch, Walter stood sentry, eyes constantly watching the horizon for the Spanish or French ships.

Suddenly on the horizon, Walter could see masts coming out of the fog, he rang the bell on deck and the drummers began to beat to quarters. As if on autopilot, Walter ran to the gunner's deck. As he loaded the canon, his mind wasn't there.

…

Fear was coursing through his body again, sped up by the adrenaline that had been released. His mind couldn't settle, it was conjuring up painful memories and images, fear of not seeing his wife or baby again, and he was ashamed to realise an overriding fear of dying, dying and not seeing them again, not being able to explain what happened. The anger that that might happen. The joy of finally being able to help defend his home country. Again, the over-riding sense of fear, fear of what was to happen. The fear of dying, without an explanation to his wife and baby. Their confusion of what happened, why he hadn't come back. That fear of dying.

As Walter watched, a canon blast came from the head of the Spanish fleet. Tt came towards Walter and *BANG*…

Dreams?

What are dreams
If not windows to your soul,
Your inner most fears and desires?

Are dreams told,
Secrets or not?
Do they lose their power
If revealed too soon?

There is power in dreams,
More than is known,
Historically told,
Dreams tell the future and the past.

Futures made,
Futures revealed,
Dreams can show the way forward.

Should we trust
In our dreams?
Some feel so real,
You toss and turn,

But do not wake.

We dream all night,
But don't always remember;
Significance is key.

Dreams that scare,
Dreams of joy,
Those that hold clues,
Those we remember.

Dreams—the window to the soul,
Your inner-most fears and desires,
Significance is key,
Terror or joy,
The ones we remember.

The Hidden Element
of Anxiety

Anxiety,
Why do I feel anxious?
Will it ever go away?

Responsibility, responsibility,
Even if it's not directly given,
Taken on nonetheless.

Need to let go, let go,
Take time for me,
So much in my head.

In my safe space,
No judgement here,
But still anxiety pops up its head.

What if they decide I'm not doing enough?
What if they think I'm not good enough?
That phrase, *What if?*

What if, what if,
Even though I know it's not true,
I still think.

Surely one day, they would have had enough,
One day, they will say, 'We're sorry but...'
Then what?

Pushing myself,
It doesn't help,
Because deep down, I know they won't do that.

Sometimes, I feel like my head will explode,
Most times, I feel fine,
No one would know.

But,
Every so often, anxiety pops up its head,
'Don't forget me,' it says.

Then the whole cycle starts up again;
Anxiety, anxiety,
That's my name.

Waterdrop

A drop
Becomes a river
in the Scottish Highlands.

torrents uisge,
sruthadh gu furasta,
tro na,
Gàidhealtachd na h-Alba.

One wee drop
Begins to carve
A river bed,
Wending and winding
Through the unforgiving landscape.

torrents uisge,
sruthadh gu furasta,
tro na,
Gàidhealtachd na h-Alba.

Millennia it takes,
One drop becomes thousands,

All following
The carved path.

torrents uisge,
sruthadh gu furasta,
tro na,
Gàidhealtachd na h-Alba.

All rivers lead to the sea,
That one wee drop
Possesses the power
To tear rock and move earth.

torrents uisge,
sruthadh gu furasta,
tro na,
Gàidhealtachd na h-Alba.

A drop
Becomes a river
In the Scottish Highlands.

Stuck in Limbo
(For Those Lost but
Not Forgotten)

Stuck in limbo,
Limbo, limbo, limbo
How did it happen?

Why am I in limbo?
What have I done?
It's like being stuck in a deep hole,
Easy to slip and slide in,
Hard to get out.

I am stuck,
Stuck in limbo,
I can hear one side,
And then the other.

I can't be heard though,
Stuck in the place,
Between places.

It's like a cupboard,
Locked and bolted,
I can hear,
But no one else can.

Limbo, limbo
A dance to many,
What can I do
If I can't be heard?

I shout, nothing,
Shall I whisper?
Life is loud,
Quiet might work.

Finally, I'm heard,
Because I'm needed,
I tried loud,
But subtle worked.

A scent wafting,
A forgotten whisper,
That good feeling,
So often mingled with sadness,
Always appreciated.

I'm leaving limbo now,
Purpose served,
I'm always here though,
Subtly in the background,
Limbo, limbo, limbo.

The Pharaoh's Curse

Where oh where to begin?

It is such an outrageous story that it is quite unfathomable, but here goes…

Date: 14 March 1922

Dear Professor Pepper,

As you are no doubt aware, there have been several archaeological digs being funded in the Egyptian province of Cairo. Your name has been one of great interest to myself and my esteemed colleagues as an eminent professor of Egyptian history. We would be honoured if you could join us as we begin to explore the hidden wonders at the complex of the Great Pyramids of Giza (known locally as the Giza Necropolis). Accommodation and travel have been booked in your name and the details will be sent forthwith. We will also include an itemised itinerary for the duration of your stay.

Awaiting your arrival on Friday, 28 April 1922, as the dig will commence on Monday, 1 May; this will give you time to acclimatise yourself to the searing Egyptian heat.

Yours sincerely,
Professor C Burcke

I had, of course, been avidly following the progress of the dig in every newspaper that I could get my hands on. without further ado, I hurried across to the telegraph office and wired my answer back to Professor Burcke. With a week to go before my departure to Cairo (which would take approximately a week and a half), the promised itinerary arrived along with a travelling schedule. I was booked on a train from St Pancras station bound for Dover. When I would arrive in Dover, I would board a ferry to Calais, France. Upon arrival in Calais, I would take a train to Paris; once in Paris, I had a sleeping berth reserved to take me to Athens. the penultimate leg of the journey was a ferry ride to Alexandretta and finally a two-to-three-hour barge trip to Cairo.

According to the itinerary, I would be spending six months in Cairo, carefully documenting all finds and photographing finds of particular interest, corresponding with the curator at the Museum of Egyptian Antiquities. It was the chance of a lifetime.

When I arrived at St Pancras, I had just enough time to buy several paperback novels and a guidebook to Cairo. My spine tingled with excitement as the train chugged into life, steam billowing from the chimney at the front of the train and the unmistakeable shrill hoot. I was finally on my way.

The train journey to Dover was pretty unremarkable. When I alighted from the train, I was immediately hit with the salty tang in the air. In the distance, I could see the dock. My ferry was yet to dock so instead of hailing a hansom cab I gathered up my luggage and made my solitary way through the small winding streets. Stopping en route at a small local bakery, I purchased several warm rolls and some pats of butter, for my stomach had been growling incessantly for the past half an hour. I could see the funnels of the ferries coming closer, I hastily finished my breakfast and continued on my way. At the dock, I showed my travel documents and corresponding ticket. To my surprise, my luggage was whisked up the gangplank, and I quickly followed along in its wake. The steward turned down a corridor and carefully deposited my luggage in a strong room. I was given a sheet of paper that showed that my luggage was being stored, along with an itemised breakdown, in-case of loss of property. I was advised by a very helpful steward to make my way outside so that I could watch the launch and wave my goodbyes. As I had been one of the first passengers to alight the ferry, I had almost imperceptibly gained a most favourable spot on the deck from which I could watch the goings on around me.

Almost three hours later, the ship's horn sounded and there was a flurry of activity on the dock side. As I watched, the ropes were unwound from the cleats on the floor and a clinking sound told me that the anchor was being brought up. A deep rumbling in the very bowels of the ship indicated that the engines were working. The horn sounded again and we began to move. We were being manoeuvred into position by a team of tug boats, they would accompany us to the mouth of the port. I had imagined that it would be a lovely calm crossing in which I could stroll along the decks, perhaps sit on a sun-lounger and watch the world go by; unfortunately, the reality was somewhat different. I felt sea-sick within half an hour of leaving dock, I stood clammy and sweating, tightly gripping the railings. As I tried to move off, I swayed and felt myself fall. When I woke, I found myself on a bunk, being attended to by the ship's doctor, who informed me that I had been taken with an acute case of sea-sickness. He advised that I stayed on the bunk, and that my luggage would be brought up forth-with. I spent the rest of the voyage curled up on the bunk trying to imagine the wonders of Egypt, hoping the thought would sustain me.

It was an arduous two-hour journey. As I had fallen ill on the voyage, I was among the first off the ferry. My luggage was carried down for me and carefully packed onto a carriage that would take me to Paris, to catch my connecting train across to Athens. The carriage journey was rather un-eventful, I was still feeling the aftereffects of my bout of sea-sickness so I slept for most of the journey, gently lulled by the soporific movement of the carriage.

Oh, how I wished that I could spend more time in Paris, the city of love, after all. Alas, it was not possible. I barely made it to my connecting train, the carriage driver was apologising profusely as he had made a wrong turn, which led us on a much longer route than necessary.

The carriage drew up outside the station and in halting French, I explained the situation, *"Mon bon monsieur je m'excuse que nous sommes à peine à l'heure, mais c'est avec la plus grande urgence que je prends ce train."*

The guard looked at the ticket and then upon examination of the letter, he leapt into action. Removing my luggage from the carriage, I was personally escorted across the station and helped aboard the train.

I gave the guard a hefty tip and said, *"Beaucoup, merci beaucoup mon bon monsieur."*

A full 10 minutes late, the train bound for Athens clacked and jolted into movement, alerting me to the fact that we were departing Paris. The journey the Athens would take three days; luckily, I had brought a few paperback novels with me. After a cursory peruse around my day and night cabins, both were lovely and spacious, with plenty of light, I stood for a moment just watching the world go by when there was an almighty growling sound. I started and spun 'round on my heel expecting to see a bear or something of that ilk but there was nothing there. The growling sounded again and I shot over to the window to check the surrounding countryside— again nothing. The third time I heard it, it was accompanied with a rumbling feeling in my stomach so I exited my cabin, locked the door and made my way down the train to the dining cart for an early dinner.

The food in the dining cart was exquisite, perfectly cooked and a varied variety. I was informed that each night there would be a special menu of delicacies from the surrounding area. Indeed, that first night I dined on escargots au beurre d'ail, Coq au Vin, and finally planche à fromage et biscuit. I headed back to my cabin for a good wash and a read.

As the train continued on its laborious journey, I lit a candle and made to close the drapes. As I looked up to tug them shut, I saw the moon; bright, shining and full. It looked like it had been magnified ten-fold, and surrounded by millions of twinkling stars. I stopped closing the drapes and just stared at the sight in front of me. The sky wasn't nearly clear enough to see this from my cramped flat in London. I sighed sadly as the familiar tug of home-sickness threatened to come crashing down over me. As the emotions came flooding forwards, I consciously began thinking of the adventure that was awaiting me in Cairo, and the feelings once again subsided. I finished closing the drapes and settled down in my sleeping cot and read a few pages of my novel.

The next thing I knew, bright rays of early morning sunshine were peeping through the drawn drapes, my paper-back was lying on the floor and I was curled up in a warm ball at the centre of the bed. I sat up and yawned, stretched and ambled into the bathroom to get ready for the day. One hour later, I was ready to face the day.

I followed my fellow passengers down the jolting train towards the dining car. After a light breakfast, I found myself a quiet nook in the tiny onboard library. From an inside pocket of my satchel, I extracted an ancient jar with a stopper of falcon-headed Qubehsenuef on it and the accompanying letter Professor Burcke sent to me. It had arrived by last post on the day before my departure. Inside was a strange note and this piece of papyrus.

Dear Professor Pepper,

It is with some trepidation that I am writing to you now, I hope this reaches you before you leave for Cairo. As I'm sure you're aware the ancient Egyptians were infamous for laying traps and curses on their tombs and pyramids, whilst we were excavating an interior corridor, we came across this scroll (please see enclosed scroll). We consulted our local on-site interpreter but he refused to translate the scroll. Indeed, he went white and began to sweat. Before departing in high dudgeon, he recited a prayer of protection. We haven't seen him since. I was loathe to speak of this before you arrived, however, circumstances dictate otherwise. Many of our dig staff have left or been taken ill during the intervening time. I implore you, please, translate this scroll for me so that I can retain the rest of my dig team and be ready for the grand opening in three months' time.

Yours sincerely,
Professor C Burcke

I can't lie, I was baffled and intrigued. Luckily, I had packed my translation book that documented both ancient text and new text, depending on the era. As I traced my fingers lightly over the papyrus, a faint smell of must and damp permeated the air; only to be expected, the pyramid hadn't been disturbed in thousands of years. As I looked at the papyrus, my imagination went into over-drive and I could imagine the scribe poring over the scroll and painstakingly drawing the characters that formed the curse in front of me.

It took me most of that second day traveling to translate the scroll. A waiter brought me a sandwich and a pot of a local blend of tea, which sustained me until dinner that evening. Just as the candles were being lit, I placed my pen down and stretched. Rubbing my eyes, I surveyed the finished translation with a slight hint of pride. I laid the translation next to the original hieroglyphs and had a final peruse over the scrolls.

'Allow this, my curse, to be unleashed and spread, a plague shall be visited on all who entered the pyramid. Fire shall rain from the skies and the Great Nile shall rise to join the sands. Thief or stranger, you have been warned.'

Satisfied that I had translated the scroll correctly, I rolled them both up together and put them safely at the bottom of my satchel to show to Professor Burcke when I arrived in Cairo. That night, as I lay in my bunk, I felt uneasy at the translation. It appeared that at least the beginning of the curse had begun to come true. Indeed, if this was the case, how long would it be before the remainder of the curse became true? Unable to shake the feeling of uneasiness that had settled across my shoulders like a cloak, I lit the lamp above my head and busied myself with one of the novels I had brought with me. Sleep evaded me that night and as a result, I stumbled through the last leg of the train journey in a haze of tiredness.

I ate sparingly at dinner, and on advice from a fellow traveller ordered a cup of warm milk infused with fragrant spices of cinnamon and clove. I had been assured that it would send me off for a deep and dreamless sleep. I hoped that would be the case, as the previous night every time I had closed my eyes, my mind was plagued with visions of fire and water. I hoped this was not a premonition of what was to come.

The visions that had plagued me the previous night thankfully were not a recurring experience and I felt rather more refreshed when I awoke. Over breakfast, an announcement was made declaring that we would be arriving in Athens at 11 am. I looked at the mantlepiece clock and saw that I had a little over an hour to be ready to depart the train.

Taking a last sweeping look at my cabin, I picked up my bags and made my way off the train. My ferry from Athens to Alexandretta wasn't until the evening so I had some time to sightsee. I joined a tour group and wiled away the time until my ferry by exploring the Parthenon and old Olympic grounds. It was fascinating, but my mind kept wandering back to the curse and how the signs and symptoms were beginning to show.

Determined to not be rushing around again, I arrived at the docks just as the gangplanks were being lowered, making me the first passenger onboard. As the ferry ride was only about four hours, there were several rows of benches on the deck. I settled myself down on one of the benches close to the railings so that I could watch the water (I found it made me feel less seasick).

Over the next 30 minutes or so, I watched the benches fill up with passengers. Finally, the gangplank was raised and a horn blared to let other boats know we were about to depart. As the deckhands untied the ropes securing the boat to the dock, a loud shout made everyone turn around. A man was standing on the dock-side waving both arms and gesticulating to the deckhands. One of them jumped off the ferry and pulled it in towards the dock so that the man could board safely, money exchanged hands and I was joined on my bench by the mystery man.

The Mediterranean Sea was relatively calm and the stern of the boat cut through the waves with ease. I concentrated on watching the waves roll and roil below me. I became quite absorbed in it until I realised with some trepidation that the mysterious man was watching me quite intently. I turned my gaze upon him and met his eyes un-flinchingly, he merely smiled at me. Perhaps my reaction was borne from outrage, perhaps the hypnotic quality of his eyes, I'm still unsure; whichever the reason, I refused to turn my gaze away. The mysterious man merely chuckled and extended his hand as though to shake mine. As if on autopilot, I met his hand halfway. The palm of his hand was calloused and leathery but firm; we shook hands. I had no need to introduce myself as the stranger said, "Julie Pepper, I presume, the eminent Professor of Egyptian History; it is an honour to meet you. I am Professor Gerard Tryton, esteemed archaeologist and Head of the History faculty at Cambridge University. Forgive me my dramatic arrival, but I had the catch you before you arrived in Alexandretta, to warn you about the curse sweeping the dig site. Already half the dig staff have been taken ill with an un-known disease, the ones who are left are threatening a walk-out if the pyramid isn't closed and the dig forgotten about. Professor Burcke is at his wits end. I know he sent the scroll to you in hopes that you would be able to translate the hieroglyphs."

I nodded, reaching into my satchel to retrieve the scroll but Professor Tryton grabbed my wrist and shook his head once.

"Not here," he muttered, glancing around uneasily.

He squeezed my wrist and let go, gesturing with his other hand. I looked into the distance and saw the shadowy outline of Alexandretta set against a blood-red sunset.

His breath tickled my ear as he whispered, "Curses have more power at this time, especially so close to their origins, we must wait until morning."

I blanched as I realised the implication of what I had been about to do. Returning my gaze to the waves below, we finished the journey in silence.

Stepping onto the jetty in Alexandretta, I filled my lungs with the hot desert air and excitement tingled and coursed through my veins. The barge that had been chartered for the final leg of the journey was waiting at the end of the jetty. Together, Professor Tryton and I boarded. Free from prying ears, we were able to talk candidly of the problems on the dig. I was interested to discover that the symptoms of the workers appeared to be closely linked to that of Malaria. Suddenly, a bell tolled and I glanced around, it was there that I had my first glimpse of Cairo. Even shrouded in darkness it was hard to miss the grandeur; I couldn't wait for the sun to rise.

As it was so late, the captain graciously allowed us to spend the night on the floor of the barge. I slept instantly and was awoken by the cries and shouts of bazaar sellers. Jumping to my feet, I gazed in awe at the liveliness and colours of the bustling crowds. Wandering through the bazaar, I took in the strange sights, sounds and smells that flooded my senses. Spices and incense infused the air. Egypt was everything I had been promised and more.

Grinning at my wonder, Professor Tryton, took me by the elbow and attempted to guide me through the hustle and bustle of the bazaar. However, with so many sights and curiosities, our progress was slow; I wanted to stop at every stall, such wonders I had never seen. Although sorely tempted, I resisted the urge to buy everything I saw. My resolve was tested to the limit when we rounded the last corner of the bazaar and came upon a table of talismans and protection potions. I knew that the potions were coloured water mixed together to sell to tourists; no, it was the talismans that I was interested in. The one that caught my eye in particular was 'the eye of Horus', an ancient symbol of protection. The scroll and the curse that had been unleashed was very much in the forefront of my mind. Deciding that I needed protection that was as powerful as the curse appeared to be, I began to haggle the price of the talisman.

Twenty minutes later and very pleased with the price I had got, we left the bazaar and made our way towards the base camp. The sun was high in the sky and blazing over our heads. Professor Tryton suggested that we find a café to go to, so that we could shelter from the midday sun. In the coolness of the café, Professor Tryton explained that the heat of the day could reach highs of 40 degrees Fahrenheit, so most people retreated to the coolness of cafés or shaded rooms.

As we sat sipping our coffee (a dark sludge like concoction that we sweetened with honey), we chatted more about our academic careers. Professor Tryton, I found out, was from the small coastal village of Devon. He had left at the age of sixteen to go to London where he became fascinated by the Ancient Egyptians (having attended a lecture at the Natural History Museum). Dropping out of his law degree, Professor Tryton switched courses to ancient history and majored in Egyptian history twelve years ago. Since then, he had written two academic papers.

Professor Tryton was equally interested to hear about my own fascination with the Egyptians which had been fostered from a young age when I would accompany my parents to dig sites and dusty tombs. My favourite but most revered memory of that time was the trip we took to Mesopotamia (just six months before I went to university). This was the trip that I was allowed to go solo, and have my own dig place. After weeks of careful excavation, I had discovered a top step. It took another four months and the rest of the team to uncover a full set of stairs leading down to a trap door. It was there that a hidden tomb was unveiled. My name had shot into the press (as I had discovered the steps first), and I arrived at university under unwanted notoriety of having discovered that cursed tomb.

As the sun began to fade and the searing heat dissipated, we began to make our way to the base camp. It was slow going, however, as the market had begun to pack away and the traders flooded the streets in front of us. As dusk became night, we found ourselves on the edge of the Giza Necropolis. Flaming lanterns lit the wooden walkway that had been erected to allow easy transportation of tools. Just next to the walkway, there was a small wooden hut, from which a short and balding security guard emerged. He looked us up and down with obvious distaste, and then in heavily accented English, he abruptly asked, "Where is your id badges? No visitors to site, it after dark, big boss say no visitors. You must leave know. Go!"

He even went as far as to try and gesture us off with the point of his rifle. At the point of being run-off by a very haughty security guard, a harsh bark of a voice cracked through the air like a whip. "Mister al-Busiri, I do hope you are not keeping Professor Burcke's most honoured guests waiti…"

We saw a large, heavily built man with a ramrod straight back come striding over to the hut. As he surveyed the scene of the guard pointing his rifle at us, he stopped dead and let off a violent volley of Arabic that sent the guard scurrying back into his hut. I looked quizzically at Professor Tryton who had given a barely imperceptible shiver. As I leant forward intending to ask if he was OK, he seemed to pull himself together and he moved forwards to meet the new guard who introduced himself as Captain Cox. He apologised profusely for the incompetency of the other guard and gave us his assurances that he wouldn't be there in the morning. We were both assigned dig passes that would allow us full access to the site.

Captain Cox accompanied us down to the tented area and showed us to our respective tents. Left on my own at the mouth of my tent, I took a deep breath of the dusty, humid Egyptian air and looked to the star-strewn sky. I fingered the amulet around my neck and muttered the words to an old protection mantra that I had been taught at my mother's knee; it would, she said, keep me safe from bad juju. As I went back to my tent, I saw in the flickering light of the dying fire Captain Cox come striding out of Professor Tryton's tent, looking livid. I stepped back into the shadows.

As he came storming past me, I heard him muttering, "…taking advantage, he doesn't have to work with these idiots. Should have said no, stupid idea. Why can't he steal the translations?" As I tried to retreat further, my foot snagged onto guy ropes on my tent, sending me crashing backwards.

As I blacked out, I heard Captain Cox's crunching footsteps and a low whisper in my ear, "My, my, someone has heard more than they needed to."

I awoke in a dimly lit room. With a groan, I tried to move my hand up to rub my forehead but I was unable to. I tried to look down but again found that I couldn't. I could hear voices behind me. In my peripheral vision, I could see flames dancing and shadows leaping up and down the stone walls. Suddenly, Professor Tryton appeared in front of me, but he looked different somehow. He was wearing a cold smile and had lost his glasses. When he spoke, I felt a cold shiver run down my spine, leaving my legs feeling like jelly. I felt that I would surely fall forwards but something was preventing me.

"Ahh, Julie, you are awake. I'm sure you have many questions and there will be time for that later. For now, I feel I must make you aware of your current um… predicament."

An evil smile lit his features, making him look, in this flickering quality of light, quite mad.

"You are currently bound head to foot against a sacrificial stone. When I have finished talking, my Anubis will come forward to remove your tongue and begin the timely job of mummification." He smiled again, allowing time for my death sentence to sink in.

Information seemed to moving slowly through my sluggish brain.

"Ahh, yes, you're currently under the influence of and feeling the effects of a very powerful knock-out drug, designed to make you compliant and non-combative but not strong enough to stop you feeling pain."

And as if to demonstrate this, he casually got his knife and drew the tip down my forearm. As I screamed, he chuckled. Somewhere in my foggy memory that laugh clicked into place and I managed to grind out, "You–were–in–Mesopotamia… Got–kicked–out for–stealing–artifacts–not–Tryton… Porter, James Porter–leaked–story–about curse–jealous of–parents'– success, not good–enough…"

My words caused James Porter to flush a blotchy blackcurrant colour. "It's no matter," he said dismissively.

"You won't be around much longer to tell anyone." With that, he signalled to someone in the shadows.

A chanting sound filled my ears, and I saw Anubis move towards me with a wickedly sharp knife and tongue pincers. On instinct, I clamped my eyes and mouth shut, praying that I was in some sort of nightmare and that by breathing calmly, I could wake myself up.

Gradually, the rapid beating of my heart subsided and I risked a look at my surroundings. I could still hear movement behind me then suddenly, I felt myself being tipped back. In panic, I screamed, forgetting the very real threat of my tongue being cut out. No clamp came down though and no agonising pain of the knife. Slowly, I realised that I was being moved. A squeaking noise to my left told me I was on a set of wheels. Deeper and deeper through passages and tunnels I was wheeled. Finally after an age, we came to a stop in a cavernous room that held in its centre a magnificent sarcophagus. I was jilted forwards as I was unceremoniously deposited in the room. I tried to speak but a piece of rag was stuffed roughly into my mouth and I was left alone, facing what I was sure was my final resting place.

For all I knew, it could have been hours or minutes later, I heard movement again behind me. Futilely, I tried to struggle. As I did, I stumbled forwards away from the stone. My legs, suddenly weak, collapsed from under me and I slumped to the floor. From my prone place on the floor, I saw a scroll dropped and a pair of legs leaving. After an age, I was able to sit up without collapsing right back down again. I tore the rag from my mouth and looked at my surroundings. Apart from the scroll, my backpack had been tossed in the corner; it was to this I went first. Almost crying with relief, I found my canteen of water and torch inside, as well the rope and knife. In the front pocket was my translation of the scroll and 'Eye of Horus' amulet. Slipping this around my neck, I next went to the dropped scroll. On it was a hastily written letter.

Professor Pepper,

I cannot guarantee you much time, I only hope that you can navigate this pyramid quickly. It may be that James Porter is taken in with my other mummy, but I am not hopeful. I despise the part I played in your well-publicised finding of the cursed tomb and now your subsequent kidnap and 'death'. BEWARE though, this pyramid holds a great curse. Use the scroll you translated, it may well be the difference between life and death. Keep your amulet close and good luck.

A friend.

Gripping the amulet in my hand, I yet again muttered my protection mantra. Setting off at a fast albeit cautious pace, I left the room and made my way down the passageway. I was all too aware of the labyrinthine structure of the inside of the pyramid; however, all my reading and study didn't prepare me for the maze I now had to navigate. As I walked, I tried desperately to rack my brain for any piece of forgotten information. Suddenly, an arrow whizzed past me at a hair breadth from my cheek and I stopped dead, not moving a muscle. Slowly and carefully, I looked at the ground and out of the corner of my eye, I saw a depressed stone, raising back into place. Upon the ground was a pattern of cream- and green-coloured stones. The stone that had just risen up was cream. Cautiously, I crouched down and gently pressed the cream stone to my left. Ducking my head quickly, I heard a whizzing noise overhead and my suspicions were confirmed. The cream stones (of which there were far more) were booby-trapped. From my crouched position, I planned my route.

I had heard the stories of arrows laced with poison that could burn you from the inside out and was loath to find out if they were true. With my heart beating a violent tattoo in my chest, I began to methodically to make my way across the room; hopping, jumping and stretching across the gaps in-between, finally arriving at the edge of the room and stepping across the threshold into a new passageway.

Making sure that I was being more watchful, I continued on my journey. I spied a fork in the junction as I came up the passage. Somewhere in the back of my mind, something was telling me to take the left fork. Deciding to trust my gut instinct, I veered left and continued on my way. As I stepped into the new passageway, the ground shook and the ceiling above my head began to rapidly descend. I threw myself sideways and rolled away as the door came crashing down with thundering finality. The crushing darkness and silence pounded in my eardrums and through the gloom I tried to make my way; one hand tracing the wall, the other groping in front of me. After what felt like an age, I rounded another corner and into a dimly lit anti-chamber. The whole room was covered in hieroglyphs, describing the occupant's journey into the afterlife. In the centre stood a magnificent sarcophagus covered in a shroud of gold. Fingers trembling, I lightly traced the hieroglyphs that were etched into the front. They spoke of a life and death, and of a terrible cursed placed upon the pyramid that would be enacted if it was ever disturbed.

Suddenly, I became all too aware of my own unwanted presence in this most sacred of places. As I began to back out of the room, the torches flared into life, and I saw a shadow creeping around the wall, but the source of the shadow was nowhere to be seen. It seemed to be pointing towards an ancient box that was on its side next to the sarcophagus. As I moved across towards it, my gaze fell across a body. I backed away from the body in horror as I saw the tortured expression and melted features of a man; he was wearing a dig staff uniform. As I backed my way into a darkened corner, I looked down to my right and almost screamed. Lying slumped against the wall was James Porter, clutched in one hand was a jar, with a stopper of jackal-headed Duamutef on it. His face wore a look of immense agony and his other hand was clawing at his throat.

The shadow was becoming more agitated the longer I stood there. It was leaping around the room in a furious frenzy. Slowly, I went back towards the box and heaved it up the right way. Inside were four indentations, two were filled; jars with stoppers of human-headed Imsety and baboon-headed Hapi. I removed the jar that James Porter had and put it back and finally I placed the jar I had in the last resting spot so that the four sons of Horus were back together. The shadow stopped dancing and rose away from the wall and slowly came down and went through the top of the sarcophagus, an audible sigh rang through the room and a golden light shone out of the sarcophagus.

As the light dimmed, a woman stepped forward and bowed deeply at me. She smiled and beckoned me forward. As I stepped into the light, an unearthly sound filled my ears and the voice thanked me for ending the years of purgatory that her spirit had endured. The light intensified and as I closed my eyes, I became aware of the sound of stone against stone. My eyes snapped open as the entrance to the room slowly disappeared.

In a haze, my ears became aware of the sound of rushing water, my head whipped 'round towards the source of the noise, I saw water pouring in from a hatch in the wall. Trying to fight the rising panic in my chest, I desperately looked for any way out. As the water steadily continued to rise, I began to float, forcing myself to lay on my back and breathe deeply. I watched the ceiling come closer. As I took one final breath and submerged myself, a cracking sound resonated through the water and I felt myself getting caught in a riptide as I was dragged through a hole in the wall.

Shock coursed through my veins and I blacked out.

A feeling of freedom ran through my soul as I drifted along in the currents of the air. I could see a body below me. As if by the power of that thought I appeared above this body and the shocking realisation hit me as I understood it was my body. I looked at my hands and I could see through them; I looked back at my body and could see the life draining from it as my hands became more solid. As I watched, my body washed up on the bank of the Nile, next to the dig site.

My body was found by a washer woman, who immediately called Professor Burcke. My ID was still visible on my chest, and my body was carefully carried from the bank and laid in the medical tent. I floated along next to myself, willing them to hurry up as my ethereal self became more solid with each passing moment. My body was covered in piles of blankets and the doctor began CPR compressions.

With each compression, I felt a tug back towards my body…
1, 2, 3, 4…

My eyes snapped open and I took a gasping breath, coughing up all the water in my lungs. My breath was coming in shuddering gasps, and I was rushed to the local hospital to be treated for shock and hypothermia. I was discharged three weeks later. James Porter's body and the body of the guide were washed up on the banks of the Nile as well, although they weren't as lucky as I was. The dig staff had all returned to the dig site the morning I was found. All traces of the mysterious illnesses had gone and everyone who was ill had come through and were alright again.

I have been back in England for three months now, I happily spent my six months in Egypt sorting through artifacts and liaising with the museum's curator to discuss how the items should be displayed. I have now been employed on a part-time basis by the British Museum to help catalogue and re-display their Egyptian catalogue.